THE UNAVOIDABLE MAN

The Unavoidable Man

BARRY DEMPSTER

Quarry Press

The publisher thanks The Canada Council and the Ontario Arts Council for assistance in publishing this book.

Several of these poems have appeared previously in *Antigonish Review*, *The Fiddlehead*, *More Garden Varieties 2*, *New Quarterly*, *Poetry Canada Review*, *Quarry*, *Somewhere Across the Border*, *Toronto Life*, *Waves*, *White Wall Review*, and *Zymergy*.

The author would like to thank Karen Ruttan, Lois and Glenn Hayes, Bob Hilderley, Roy Vanderlip, Sonja Skarstedt, and Ted Dempster for their support, encouragement and/or inspiration.

CANADIAN CATALOGUING IN PUBLICATION DATA

Dempster, Barry, 1952-
The unavoidable man

ISBN 0-919627-97-8

I. Title.

PS8557.E4827U63 1990 C811'.54 C90-090425-9
PR9199.3.D34U63 1990

Cover art entitled "Hu" by Jörg Immendorff. Reproduced by permission of Galerie Michael Werner, Köhl, and the Art Gallery of Ontario.

Design and imaging by ECW Type & Art, Oakville, Ontario
Printed and bound in Canada by Hignell Printing, Winnipeg, Manitoba.

Distributed in Canada by the University of Toronto Press, 5201 Dufferin Street, Downsview, Ontario M3H 5T8 and in the United States of America by Bookslinger, 502 North Prior Avenue, St. Paul, Minnesota 55104.

Published by Quarry Press Inc., P.O. Box 1061, Kingston, Ontario K7L 4Y5 and P.O. Box 348, Clayton, New York 13624.

for Brian

✛ ✛ ✛

We are not permitted to linger, even with what is most intimate. From images that are full, the spirit plunges on to others that suddenly must be filled; there are no lakes till eternity. Here, falling is best. To fall from the mastered emotion into the guessed-at, and onward.

— R.M. Rilke

Contents

WILD MEN

HOLDING FATHER

The
Body
Recovers

TO WAKE THE DEAD

Comes the Father followed by
a cortege of sleepy sinners.
Stone-cold church gaping
like an empty tomb. Eyes steaming
in the stained glass light.

Death is said to slowly climb
the esophagus, disguised as
a kind of hunger for nothing
on earth. Premonitions of death
occur frequently on Sunday mornings,
the heart chilling to the hardness
of wood. Lips barely moving
as the Bible tells the future.
Time reflected on cathedral ceilings,
a constriction of clouds.

Father filled with salvation,
the present moment caught
in his throat. Bully this,
confess to that, he slaps
his congregation's soul
the way a surgeon beats
on a broken heart. *Careful,*
Christ is slipping away with
every undetermined breath. Sounds
like the world is bound to end
before the Sunday roast is even
browned. The only thing to do
is hold each muscle still, pretend
to be a pillar or a pew. Father's
voice passes over row on row, the
awful radar of an angel's sword.

How words can terrify. Speak of
God at the right moment
and the room will seethe
with everlasting dread. Father
never seems to stop and
swallow. His sermons hit the floors
and scale the walls. As if
he were trying to wake the dead.

THE BEGINNING OF THE END

I

February, the sky wanes, grey
like the marble eyes of statues;
cold, the gulls stiff above the bay
the shape and tenure of a bruise.
Along the crisp and paling beach,
below the power plant's slippery bluff,
a man or two, with dog unleashed,
iced pebbles strewn black and rough.

May, the crooked sky falling
like a shattered windowpane;
warm, the gulls clumsy, stalling
mid-air, the firm descent of rain.
On land, a soggy strip of sand,
the whining of the power site,
a man alone, a trembling hand
sunk low, a frayed and crippled kite.

August, sky retrieving glare once more
like makeup on a dead man's face;
hot, the gulls nibbling on the shore
the remnants of a season's waste.
Beyond, the driftwood twists baroque,
a flash of power plant, a spark,
a man electrified, through smoke
his burning hands swept high and dark.

November, the sky bitter, black
like the dark side of a mirror;
numb, the bones of gulls charred and cracked,
trampled on cluttered sand, a smear.

Nowhere the bay, the pebbles, lost,
the power plant a faint grey glow,
no man about, the limits crossed,
the seasons scattered high and low.

2

Streets in shambles: pissy trees
and ribcage cats, children buttoned
into garbage bags, mousy clouds.
The end is near.

Sitting on top of a telephone
pole, I watch for a full profile
of November. A supersensible gloom.

Wouldn't it be grand to grab
a grey breeze, swimming spider-legs
with autumn scum. To be part
of the fog, not fogged.
Some solitary pilot above it all
dipping rusted wings in wires and leaves,
a fuming elegy for the gravity of light.

A backward glance at summer,
the shoot of a sharp green pin.
Turn away, turn away,
the past is a mollusc's mirage
trapped in the hinge of an eye.

I climb down from my pole,
end this waiting game of seasons.
The trees are losing birds wholesale.
Children's smiles yellow on their thumbs.
I set my gloomy face beneath a cloud,
winterized, lengthy as a shadow.

3

Outside my window, back yards
reproduce themselves: fences separating
one from one, like spines.
December mud, rusting barbecues,
injured leaves, all are bleeding
uncontrollably. Squirrels gallop in the air,
starlings bang their heads on frozen twigs.

My orange cat shames the patio with
a furry burst of light. Dead marigolds
pose marble in the frost. The fence, like
all fences, stiffly stares down the world.

This day is all window;
December's habit of dying evenly.
Sad, muddy eyes divide the world
in plots, then weep for loss, for
differences. Each poplar tree browns
alone, each blade of grass withers.

My window watches a street of windows
while my fence holds forever in its slats.

THE WORKING DEAD

This is the realm of blind potatoes.
Ingrown afterlife: stuck here in grips
of gloves and garden tools, grasping
underground cables for filaments of warmth.

Maggot fear is luxury, as are
worms and suffocation. No-one
is digging to Tibet. A mouthful
of loneliness, an incision of air.

The valor in death is inorganic.
Inside the machine: the tiny
courage of bolts and seeds. Rooted,
used, an eternal hum of grief.

Absorbing wars and feet, we are
the guts of tulips, of telephones
and beans. The foundation of now.
Shovels, vaults and dreams.

Here are the witch's ashes, cooled
and mixed with green forgotten gems.
Here are the lost cats, the basement
windows, the discarded carrot tops.

This is the land of bitter onions.
Crying upside down: forced to grow
your grass and graceless houses, grumbling
as your children highrise closer to the clouds.

THE WAITING ROOM

Waiting in a waiting room —
would-be nurses, waiters,
dignitaries, all of us
temporarily unemployed.
Waiting for miracles, you
know, a money tree, a
relationship. Some with
prayers as references, others
visual, the sucked-in hunger
of the streets.

One by one, we disappear,
a navy blue man
mispronouncing our names.

My heart is cracked, a
novelty bank. On good days
seven out of ten fingers
work. No need to fret,
I will not cry, but if
suddenly I cease to move,
touch me somewhere I would
never expect. There are two
sides to me, the past and this,
a pose to compliment your hands.

As we wait, no-one speaks,
like dishes in a rack. A
small display of talent, yes
one can read, another sweeps
shoulders in a glance. So neat,
I can talk to the pleat in my pants
or place a finger gently to my eye.

When my name is called
in tones of navy blue
I do not disappear but
merely change my seat, my room.

I think I shall become
a member of the human race, a
nickel branch or half
a conversation. Might you need
someone who can pray for profit,
who can feed the hungry with their
knees? Just temporary work,
waiting for the future.

ENVYING

I

Those chatoyant Carnahans, they
glimmer greenly in splendid gowns,
growing gold when the sun slides down.
Come dark, their eyes go up in flames.

Big Daddy Carnahan dreams of
public opinion. Madame stirs
for what's left of society.
The young tell fortunes to themselves.

Somehow the rich lead convex lives,
their wombs and spleens like points on stars.
A greening glimpse, a golden gleam,
a flex of nakedness, composed.

2

What's in a name?
The Vanderbilt's remind me
of a view, something blue
seen from something white.
Rockefeller burns while Getty dazzles,
moonlight falling from the chrome of moving cars.

The best shape is round.
A curve of lips:
syllables reuniting in the air.

The finest name drops to the grass
like a meteor, heaven
embodied in the brain.

I'd like to name myself
a tiny planet, the tip
of a tongue.

Listen, the world rotates,
repeats itself. The name is
endless, a perfect satin sound.

3

The Prokofiev piece goes nicely
with a pearl grey living room.
Symphonies and chandeliers: how
whole. An invisible orchestra
hovers over ivory chairs.
A taste of polished gold.

Come May, tulips sweeten windowsills.
Perhaps a life-sized statue of a god.
Beneath a patio umbrella
shadows sip from slender straws.

Before the gilded mirror a Cartier
splashes prisms on a scarf.
The diamonds float as if mid-air.

A bonafide collection of
senses, things. Prokofiev made
tiny as a pearl. The ever-present
colour of answered prayers.

All we see are chandelier shadows,
a mirror on fire with flawless light.
A glimpse of flowered windowpanes.

All we see are things
in our search for reflections.
Things like scarves and ivories,
like men and gods.
O shaded eyes. O want.

4

In dreams, he shakes his money trees,
a storm of dollar bills.
Up to his waist in greed.

No more the little man,
the tucked-in cotton sheet.
The rich overflow their needs.

Welcome to the land of desire.
Women spread on TV-beds
like stylish strands of beads.

A man begins overpowering dreams:
shaken boughs and broken limbs.
Orchards of naked trees.

5

Womens' fuzzy kisses on one another's cheeks,
silky de la Renta hues.
They are smiling the smiles of plums.

Men are covered head to toe in tans,
tuxedos, Italian shoes. The bare skin
of a handshake, the friction of wedding rings,
reminds them of glossy embraces.

Together, a murmur of love.
Silk rolled on a damp palm, skin
swishing against skin. Women with their
upper arms flushed. Men peeled to the pale bone.

May all your kisses leave rumours on the lips.
May your nudes be airbrushed in Italian shoes.
May love leap the octaves of a blush.

6

Independence is a privilege.
The self, aloof, issues forth
a splendid view . . .
time unbroken and green.
Such a man is the size
of what he sees: a distance.

The rest of us, the Toms and Harrys,
space the world through magazines.
Deliver us from need,
from blurring vision.
Let us not look past each other
on our way to emptiness.
To be seen, never truly seen.

Pose the view: a blade of grass
bragged to an emerald,
a beyond claimed as eternity.

BURNING

We burn. We run to the screams
and back, to white
arms lifted in despair and back.
                    — Donald Revell

Prometheus is struggling with the sunset —
a skirmish or a flash
of radiation.

The world below reddens nightly,
children reined to wounded stars.
Somehow fire pours between us,
a rotgut of the mind.

Hearts bleed on every continent,
heads held high, heavenly.
Swallowers of height,
inflamed brains.

Out to save mankind, man is
dressed up like a bloody rose,
a shepherd in scarlet teeth.
Fighting fire with fire.

The sons of Prometheus throw
themselves on beds of smoke
while scattered sparks
set fire to the breeze.

And the world burns, top to
bottom. Falling stars.
Ashes in the eyes, on the tongue.

How the continents grow crisp and
black. How heaven speaks with heat
instead of prayers. Full of everyman's
struggle, a man consumes
himself with death.

Prometheus vanishes in time —
periodic peace or darkness.
Empty minds. Roses
blazing underground.

MAPMAKING

Gunshot syllables: the rhythm of anthems,
islands shouting from ragged shores.

Virtue is a man who shoots only at strangers.
Be it squares, lots or maps, someone will eventually
stir the grass. The trespass of wanderlust.

Dirt is a real prize. And roots.
The wind puffs along the hairline, parting
the brain into two camps. Blasted hills.

Pastures repel pastures, rivers split
and mountains implode into caves.

The world is a self-delusion, sustained.
The world is a floating footprint,
a shadow men fall for.
Countries of mine and moss, of clutched air.

Such is the war between shut-ins and
those exposed on the barbed-wire fence.
They are fighting for the rights to snowfalls.
Sunlight squatters. The realm of a glance.

HUNGERING

Food for the spirit: strawberry
tarts and a cake made to taste
like a cloud. First the stomach's
seams start to tear, ribs disappearing
in a giant gulp. Men shedding
tongues and jaws, their fingers falling
on the pretty paper plates.
The hunger for forgiveness
bursting at the taste of Christ.

How high must a prayer rise to
truly satisfy? There are
women here with journals full
of recipes. A child who
wishes his mouth were twice its size.
Sin leaves a nasty taste for
all, a bitter emptiness.

Someone tells the flavor of manna,
a cross between the gingerbread
and the apple pie. An ounce of
laughter, the room melting with
imagination . . . how would it
really be? That rare savor of
a baby's thumb. A sweet tooth.
Taste buds lifted from the tongue.

SINGING

We file in, filling the pews
with sensible shoes. A sniff of
understated lilac perfume.
Fingertips pooling on Bibles.
The organ murmuring like the
wires in a long-distance call.

Sunday droops in its crystal vase.
This hollow church — a crack of knees
sounds deep within the wooden walls.
Stained-glass angels hide behind their
purple wings. The priest whispers things
to his wide white robe. Holy, all
as one . . . holy, the swallowed tongue.

Prayer and blessings, the voicebox
tingling at the mention of love.
A reading from the book of Luke
politely clears the throat. Soon
a sermon lilting in our ears.

Listen up, listen here, repeat
the loudness of the Lord. We
are learning how to speak in
metaphors. How to creak and roar.

Hymns, tuneless, dive from bottom lips.
Shakespeare on a binge, Cole Porter
with a limp, the words and music
rising in us. All those
trembling adjectives, haunting verbs.
Christ cracked as a high note, held.

When I sing I am not so
sensible. The soul, a bold
and noisy place. Week to week
Sunday's simple face looks up,
speaks out. No doubt the sound is
awful to the disinclined:
the twisted larynx of a saint.

But how we try, explain, express,
the hugeness of it all. Singing
to a silent God, a swallowed
faith. Singing out that ancient dream.

THE BODY RECOVERS

The body begins to flicker again.
The soul a kind of chamois
buffing the waxy brain —
health, health,
a slipknot of a hardy word,
a self-promise.
Thus spoke the future
to a reflection of itself.

But the body is a talebearer,
whispering with tides and smears.
Unsteady, it says, a collapsible chair.
The soul snags in the brain,
thoughts coarse, unclear.
Just trying to appear
the future breathes a heavy smudge.

The
History
of Love

PICTURE DESIRE

A kiss, the moon rushed off its feet,
a toppled bedroom lamp.
How desire is announced,
lips like a purple marquee,
a bruising of ecstasy.
Deep and squeezed, the slippery pose
of you and your French hips,
shadows dipped between your breasts.

All I really want to do
is be with you, a rendezvous . . .
you sigh and say your heart
is just a little lower down.

Such sweet pieces of ourselves.
Black stockings wrapped around
your ankles, my shirttail stuck
in a crease, the room haphazard
with mismatched shoes, piles of pants
and pillows flattened against the walls.

You call me your lover
or else, the man who fit
amazing parts of himself
into your favorite fantasy.
I respond with the shape of you
on my mouth, a purple word.

Dwelling in the dark recesses
of blurred desire,
no-one can tell where either
one of us begins.
Whose shadowy arms, whose
mid-air moon?

All I really want to do
is reach beyond my need
for you, a hand daring
a dark room. This is what
I want, that deep chill where
every piece of me is given up.

NO MAN'S LAND

Hand on hand: crossing the Rubicon.
Our first embrace of no man's land,
love settling in a cloud of dust.

Self-assured, I promised you
a toss of bones, a bird.
An inner place called paradise.
To lose the way in one
another: starry pioneers.
The night sustains, no fear of
boundaries, we are free as far
as wings can be, the length
and breadth of touch.

Our song is not an anthem.
Forget both fountains and fists.
Directions are simple: as the birds
swoop and fly.

Side by side, loving nations.
Embraces flatten fences, borders, walls,
our bodies rising and rolling like the hills.

SURRENDER

Surrender is almost a smell
on the tips of her naked fingers:
faded soap, sun, friendly innocence.

The man is coaxed from
his anxious cove. Heart squeezing,
sniffs and shivers. Desire pulls
and braves up, improvising fate.

In the comedy of sexes, woman
is the one with friendly fingers
dangling from the boat.

Man the curious minnow, mouthing
warily, growing familiar with those darting
rays of light. Finally takes her
small and bright. Pretending happenchance . . .
rehearsal of romance.

The perfect she: finger signals,
nonchalant.

He wants it innocent, assured.
A sleeveless sleight of hand.

LOVE PLACE

Sopping through candied heart canals,
slithering along the blue banks of the wrist,
rolling in agony on the tongue —
there is no such spot as love.

Better to stretch, spread out:
vertebrae velvet on the lips. Intoxicating
collarbones of sweat. Fingers
one by one exhaled.

Soon love is sighted everywhere,
circulation bold. It cools in
the open lap or lumps together on
the head of a nipple. It graces the pores.

Ah, the multiplicity of love.
The hairs on the back of a palm
bristle, each one a stroke, a
sweetness, a crease on the tongue.

Unpremeditated, shivers form a breast,
a thigh, an ankle. The shape
of love strains and varies.
Forever temporary, offhand.

Tonight, embrace the pancreas in a
shower of insulin, then the earlobe
which was made to fit a space between the teeth.
The buttocks, as always, will be electric.

A moment only for this — your pasture,
your other planet, your sex — whatever
the air forms. Hold it with your thighs
and feel the breath escape . . . that's love.

The isolated organ is a microscopic slide.
A moment merely a biopsy of the senses.
An orgasm breaks the webbed bones
and runs the gamut of nervy hollowness.

Love shoots the system and fools it whole.

HAND TO HAND

Such an embrace: fingers slipping through
the strings of a deep guitar.
Those bossy nerves electrified,
the body stamped by the strain of a touch.
You hold me, a cat's cradle of wire
and thumbs. You hollow me, taut
and blue. Look at the tense man
on the tightrope: look at a man's hard body
between a woman's wrists. Embraced,
the body takes the shape of a hand.

Hairs will rise, hearts reaching.
A swirl of fingerprints. An open mouth.

Such oneness: my body sliding through
its ribs and fingers, into the tenseness
of your arms. All nerves, whatever
touches touches back. This is known
as entanglement, as a disappearing act.
This is known as an absolute lack
of empty space. A man hollowed
on the wrists of a blue embrace:
a man buried in a woman's body
the shape of a string or wire.
Oneness, the body risen, the body swirled.
A tightrope reaching hand to hand.

SWALLOWED SONG

I swallow you: a snake transfigured
by the shape of its hunger.

Adam with a huge love
caught in his throat.

The tongue is connected to a heart,
a groin; kisses bonding the intimate
body. Acrobatic muscles, hollow bones.

Together, we are placeless. Elusive
possibilities. The best I can do
is bleed you a map on my skin:
blushing, bruised. The body spent and shared.

Love does not discriminate between
a lip and a nipple. In love, both are
pigments of the whole skin. No proof
exists but hunger: each devouring, disappeared.

My mouth contains you, one stray cell
sucked from the softness of your neck.
Of course, my body changes: belly
swells and arms symbolize; ankles
crack while hips rhythmically melt.
Look, love is one nakedness
made from more than enough.
That blushing shape is not misplaced;
is always there, like a huge tattoo.

There, we swallow, ah. We are
swallowed by the long night, the snaky
bed. Forever hungry for the shape of
each other, our gulping hands.

Come, love is connected to love, to
anything claimed in the name of love.
A kiss, a muscle.
The heart beats all over the body,
pulsepoints transfiguring.

This is all a love song.
From the blood. Elusive body . . .

I am a lip, you a nipple.
The snake swallows; connected,
contained, we are devoured whole.

CITY LOVING

Out the bedroom window, a bus yard
idles high; diesel fumes
filling the air with sooty roses.
Back of our house, cars
stutter through the lane.
In the distance, a train rattles,
an airplane shatters clouds.
Next door, a slurred radio, a kettle
screech, a breathless appliance.
In each other's arms, we tremble
slightly, coiled wires.
Dreams of distance, desire
connecting us to stars.
My hand on your breast makes you hum.
The whistle of my tongue.
Lower, loud, our bodies blending,
sucking, sizzling . . . all things in one.
The house empowered.
The city loving with extension cords.
Day and night, the earth moves for us,
a singleminded machine.

DRESSED TO DISAPPEAR

First the slip, then the stockings;
soon you are rustled silk,
the sun hissing on the windowsill.

Sweaters, skirts, whatever follows
shapes the day. An arm stuck mid-sleeve,
a stubborn zipper. The world bulges through.

High-heels up and down the hall.
Nervous preparation, rushed-off
radar tapping out routines.

I watch you with your coat, such
grappling. Gloves to handle subways, streets.
A purse full of passwords and paint.

Off to face the day, to beat the band.
A hiss and tap: a snake banging at the door.
Monday morning. Job-bound,
covered up, rustling beneath it all.

Left behind, I lie on the unmade bed
in my underpants. A cotton sound, a shush.
Shapeless mornings with nothing to do.
Missing you, your body dressed to disappear.

ANOTHER BREATH

At midnight you were an empress,
striptease silk and lowered eyes.
The dream danced obsessed.

Morning, magnificence tough
to relate. You are royal on
my fingertips, I say — a grateful
chuckle. Somewhere in the night
man and woman built an empire
in the springs of a vast bed.
History slowly nibbles the light.

How many moons are left for
us to breathe our fantasies?
You will be an angel stripped
of everything but wings.

Come midnight, here little shepherd girl,
bonnet trailing down your naked back.
All our possible lives: such delightful
shadows cherished in the night.

In my morning journal, write:
she was silver in my veins.
Go down in history, another
breath, an inexhaustible dream.

Wild
Men

WILD, WILD

Wild, how trees claw at one another,
rocks buried half-alive, spiders spitting
mid-air. We are not to confuse these wilds
with human pathology. Nor to let literature
weep pathetic. Wild is numb, is brainless.
Where nothing ever happens twice.

This tree is a wooden cell; it knocks
in the wind and grows. This rock is a mineral
deposit. And the spider, the most alive
we'd say (like us), is a dark enzyme
oozing in the so-called light. A man may walk
through these wilds, or he may not.
If a poet, he will probably want to tell:
the same weeping willow again and again.

Numb is somehow tender to the touch — moss,
bark, breeze. A beautiful brainless rock,
the act of sitting an act of love.
Each soft spider dashing the wrist
brings one thrill of skin alive.

Wild, how trees touch back, rocks
muscle into open hands, spiders land.
A man sits confused in the forest,
pathetically talking to himself.
Everything feels and can't forget.

All men are pathological. Weeping,
they bring the adjectives down.
Always another man, half-awake, dangling
in the air. This is man's makeup,
the literature of all kinds.
The same man tough as trees, deep
as rock, spitting dreams. Wild,
he says. Wild.

THE HARD LIFE

Who is the man who boasts
a happily married attitude
to poverty, pride
and daily ulcer pain?
Thinking about myself
causes cataplexy,
the man in the mirror
dropping out of sight
like thin air slipping
through a grasp.
How many fathers have fallen
down the cracks in a point of view?
How many have called out
from the bottom of a frozen smile?
When I'm not swearing to myself
that fate is simply an adjustment,
I'm doubled over in a dullsville
of complaints. How fond I am of
my extremes, those undemanding brags.

ALL HE SEES

The man is praying in a pair of dark glasses,
pretending to be alone.

Sending complications to God.

Something devilish snoops through the soul.
Out the doubts: the round world
only round, or is that death with
life in its mouth? Deep down Christ
is no more animated than a hologram.

The dark man confesses a spindly church,
a monotonous Bible, a displaced faith
in nuclear destruction. How can the world
rise round, still round . . . how can heaven
escape radar and astronauts?

Once upon a time a prayer was word
was ship was breeze. Spoken up.

Truth was short and sweet.

The man is thinking of his loneliness,
no more shape to life, no distant light.
Trouser knees the only holy sheen.

All he sees is world.
Where else can dark prayers go?

THE UNAVOIDABLE MAN

He is the brother-in-law who
sells life insurance, the high school
bully, the next-door neighbour
with a Black Sambo on his lawn.

His greetings bruise your upper
arms, his knowledge of hockey
numbs you. Such companionship:
candid farts and comedies
with the "little woman." The
subtlety of jabs and winks.

The guy belongs to everyone.
Like "Tie a Yellow Ribbon," he
repeats himself. Talks of cars as if
they were drugs. Brags about his boss,
bellows through his sleeves. Hollers in
the screen door, a giant water hose.

Come the family picnic,
the school reunion, the
barbecue. A basketball
to chase, retrieve. The ultimate
tale of last night's game. A
couple of gasps in the direction
of every woman's legs.

The guy and I wolf down our
paper plates, throw ourselves gassily
into conversation, take it
easy or whichever way we can.

In the dusk we trade stories
of skeet shoots and salmon streams,
killing mosquitoes and piling them
on the arms of our chairs.

LAMENTATIONS

On Donahue a woman laments
her son stricken with a mute virus;
his dead heart an unwise host.

My muscles cramp, breath in bits.
Five days into a mysterious cold,
still feeling curiously old and overtaken.
The frailty of life, that yielding
refrain: how the body simply blows away.
More than this, I am thinking of plans,
of diagrams not yet detailed, of
the future snatched away.

Outwards, the atmosphere crackles
with flickering schemes, with
lingering comet tails.

On Donahue a dozen women
dampen the cameras.
Tears phoned-in from across America.
All the dead sons are a puff of blinding light,
a magician's disappearing gloves.

A woman cries at possiblities: what if?
Grief and memory are alive and intertwined.

Absence ill-defined, never bare.
Too much left behind.

TO GRANT (A FAMILIAR VERB)

Grant, godson of Seabrights Bay, water-skis
like Christ smoothing over waves. He
flies, he veers, he writes his name
across the shore. This comes easy
for a man, one foot lifted in the air.
Except for me, clumsy cousin, jerking
on the end of a rope. I am the wet head
hiding in the lily pads, the
crayfish crouched beneath the dock.

Grant can climbswimshootfixdare, any
kind of verb. Grant can. In my dreams
he swings from sumachs while rewiring
toasters and cracking squirrels
on the rocks below. He dives through
my exclamations, my immobile ohs.

Nightly I used to dim Grant
in those braggart summer skies.
So what, can he moon or splendor?
When has the world ever needed
someone to run on the water
or rewire the trees?
In the dullest of darks,
I would lose my silhouette
in deep-thought swings and dives.

Older, slightly blurred, life
is not quite so divided. Grant still
swims the bay each morning and
is rumoured to understand the innards
of VCRs. Now it pleases me
to see something bobbing in the waves,
having something explained. Pieces of
Grant. A familiar verb.

In the cut-out past Grant is pasted
over top a paper wave, two pieces
of rope in his capable hands.
I am not in the picture, except for
the merest shadow of a scissor blade.

HAIRCUTS

Bite after bite of scissors;
my true-blue hair dies on the barber's floor.
Gelled and spiked, the man in the mirror
stings the light: a sharpened image.

Men glimpsing men, a modern curiosity
from the neck up. Boys with bristles
seem dutiful, yet immature. Strands
and flips, a laboured nonchalance.
Long in front, in back, soft or straggled,
curled, straight. Even baldness states:
a confident carelessness. My spikes
prick the eyeballs of wavy men.

In the place of handshakes, instead of
skittish punches and bony hugs, men are
glancing at one another. Admiration, imitation,
touch. My hair has a personality, like a
corduroy shirt or a car. I can run my fingers
through my best friend's scalp and know
the truth. The barber and his hairy floor,
our psychotherapy: where roots are discovered,
where parts are defined.

MEN LIKE ME

The men gape at me, a visitor
from the planet "youth," a sphere
that shows its dark side to God.
I am wearing red running shoes
and a skinny leather tie,
my hair spiked with Aqua Net.

This is the way a prodigal
Baptist boy dresses for outer space,
a place shaky with falling stars
and an overwhelming lack of weight.

Soon, the stares subside. Eternity's
attention span: intensely
short. The sad-eyed past turning
away from the bobbing future.

In California men are rumoured
to worship clothes. Long hair slinks down
awkward spines, eyes playing tricks on
the moment. Bottled blondes, big
brooches, that horrid colour pink.

Psychologists bury their
faces in self-help books; jocks
jeer from balconies; parents gasp.

Men like me, approaching thirty-five
with the certainty of computer
chips, find themselves dabbling in
jewellery drawers and religion,
donning mauve socks and prayers, thinking
a lot about death and hair.

We find ourselves in the strangest
worlds, in a galaxy called
church. Faith renewed, faith just thought about.
Old holy men hide their blurry eyes,
ask for patience with spikes and
sneakers, with all that disguise.

Together we shuffle into
hymns and parables, struggling
into shiny Sunday shoes.

THE DEATH OF ITALO CALVINO

Look, how the elegant man
suddenly sinks to the sidewalk.
Around him startled buildings rise,
a city chorus of rock and change.
He sinks into a tarry crack
the way a painted face
will fall within a frame.
One foot dangles from the curb.

In death, all cities
are gaping holes.

Look again, an elegant book
is fluttering to the pavement.
Open-paged, the words,
surprised, attract the eyes
of sinking men, of stone.
The city is described by glance.
Long ago, when cracks were wide,
a face fell invisible.
An absence others dangle from,
in search.

One man is now a crack,
surrendered to the sinking stone.
Look down, the final city
fills his place.

PICASSO'S EYES

Picasso stands at the window,
hands on the glass, watching sunset
divide the branches of a tree
into layers of broken bones.
And then beyond, a river
suspending sky, blood blue with
shimmering veins. The world is
a fragment of man, he says, a
corner of my own reflection.

Unremarkable, that
face at the window, those
hands pressed smooth as glass.
Passersby dismiss the narrow
lips, the head without a stitch
of hair, a lazy man, not
a thing to do but stare.

And yet his eyes seem much too big:
lamps lit early for the dusk,
light spilling on the busy street,
illuminating heads and feet,
diminishing the glow of sunset.
Someone whispers how they feel
as if their ribs were pierced,
those eyes like shards of glass.

He watches women, how their
arms divide from bulky breasts.
And men, how legs are long as
light, stepping up and down the
sky. Entire town seems rearranged . . .
walls sloping sharp like chins,
other windows rolling open,
sinking shut, a blinking of his eyes.

He claims a world lost in shape,
distorted in a whim of
broken light, a geometry
of shadows and resemblances.
He stays to watch the dark
emptying of streets, trees fading
in a river blind with sky. Left
to himself, his own reflection, a
face suspended in the window, like
a lamp, a moon . . . a glass eye.

EINSTEIN AT THE BLACKBOARD

Einstein sits in a small room,
before a blackboard, running
chalk through his hair like a pencil
on a notepad. Staring into
smudged darkness, he sees a blur
of numbers, not enough, a
puzzle skull of broken bones.
A planet then, those zeros,
effervescent atoms like
flecks of chalk. A tiny universe
trapped in a tiny room. Seeing
further, first the deepest black
of board, the flat edge of an
ancient world, then deeper
still, the burning white of lime,
until, until . . . another
room, another man . . . Einstein
peering through dimensions,
witnessing himself.

A line of heartbeats, a set
of blurry numbers on a
board. The surface of a planet
as smooth as slate. A man's body
begins and ends in a glance.
Look, my eyes are revolving
doors, always open on the
flat of day to day, sneaking
peeks inside, that smudge of ghost,
the burning white of soul.

Trapped within my tiny body
I stand before a mirror.
Ah, haphazard bones, those figure
eights and tall-tree ones. My eyes,
the algebra of hope. Searching
further, irises deep and
blue, the brink of sight, then further
still, pupils burning black, until . . .
reflected room . . . no matter
what dimension, depth, a man
witnesses himself
while contemplating truth.

Holding
Father

SCOTLAND IS FARAWAY

Scotland is a faraway place,
hidden in hills of burning heather,
moody with the mean North Sea.
Out of Maud, a Dempster
makes these miles, a map of Canada
crashing through the weary mist.

Grandad slipped into the body
of Toronto, a spirit flickering
in a statue's eyes.
Did Scotland die without him?
Sheep leaping blind
from golf course cliffs.

The thought of leaving home
cold in the close-up brain.
Missing millions of maples
and old Lake Ontario.
A Dempster, far out from his name,
a little misty in Grandad's grave.
Scotland, a face disappearing into stone.

HOLDING FATHER

I

He walks through a grove of crabapple trees,
slipping on and squashing the hard wine fruit.
Younger, he was a rake, curiously clawed.
Now, flat and clumsy, he breaks no ground.

Some apples still hang from wormy branches,
gnawed and puffy from the rain.
The world is no longer smooth, he claims,
but burst into slivers. Someday soon, snap,
the world will dangle, an old man clinging to a leaf.

The interval between stem and bark
is a laboured breath. Thumbs press,
lost in colourless sap.
My father plucks a crab which mushes
in his hand, wipes it on the twisted trunk.
Nothing worse than rotting summer.
Dead apples shining on a sticky branch.

Strange, the clinging. This sickly grove.
He latches on to the farmer's fence,
solid in its snaky curves.
A house can go forever,
this fence, a patio, even chairs.
A careful life contrives to simply outlast.

The orchard road is bold and dry.
Walk with me, a step, request,
walk and turn and climb.
He holds an apple in his hand,
a frail crab, good luck.
Whole it sits on his fingers like a living thing.

2

Memory is a treasure hunt
through conversations, closets,
layers of skin.

Lawrence Welk and his bubbly oompah
bring back slender dances
on the rec room floor.

The peerage of war vets and lawn-mowers,
of garage mechanics and *Look* magazines.
I can't picture him a younger man;
he can't remember the kernel of proof.

Po-faced, he has come to surrender:
his blue wedding suit,
his two-fingered whistle, his hair.
Me with my aching legs, his pacing.
Both of our shouts.
He forgets what his own father looked like,
runs to the photo album on the sly.
Wait until, he's fond of saying —
til memory is a giant rock,
the hands no longer made of TNT.
Where is the pin from Texaco?
What was 1943?

Memory is a caved-in property.
The shock of forgetting yourself.

3

The years collapse, a manslide.
Head over heart, will never stop.

A little boy flies by my father's window,
a comforting squeal, sweeping gone.
The world is raining boys of all ages,
a boast of thunder. Catch their eyes,
they are filled with the wonder of their fall.

Cousins in the treetops,
giant uncles peering from streetlamps.
That birdy teacher appears
in a cloud of coloured chalk.
The first boss, booming plentiful.
Blind dates with fingers
twirling in their hair.

A young man: Dear, Teddy, Mister.
Everyone is calling for my father,
wants and schemes,
a drift of August in the air.
Opening his first Texaco:
gasoline dreams of suburban flowerbeds.
Marrying, a colour scheme,
a kiss the length of a bed.
A son, perfect to the frequent touch.

The casual years fall slow-motion.
He is almost an eagle,
the delicious suddenness of swoops.
The house floats, the wife breezes,
the baby boy unclouds his eyes.

A middle-aged man stones by the window,
landing on a service station floor.
Money dies on trees,
rainbows stinking in the gasoline.
My father leaps on life, no sucker,
but life collapses underneath.
Ulcers, anger, the downwind hooks it all.

Fat cats, explorers, golden boys,
my father sheds personas in the beating rain.
Finally retires, a pin.
The window smokes, yet still the sound
of old men zooming by.
Time is a blur in the middle of the room;
did it happen, will it, which?

Lately my father sees bones
dropping from the sky,
strives to scare us.
Yep, saw a ghost, saw that bugger Death.
This world is nothing but a trampoline
and life's the fall.
Better to see these crazy things than be.
Look, a funny bone tumbling fast.

4

On the golf course, knocking
the rubber out of that ball.
My father bends and glares, swinging his hips.
Eyes the sun as if he'd launched an Icarus.
"Did you see that?" he calls, his grassy brag.
He can still knock hell off the beam.
Seventy-two and doing.

Lying in his lap, a kid,
his hands buried most of me.
Little chip. Little man.
"Throw me, Dad," the wind severe,
the sky blooming.
The game of serious life.

My father follows the flight
of each and every ball,
his club swooning to the green.
The way he used to look at me,
bouncing from his arms,
a confidence more precious than love.
A follow-through.

I mispronounce his longings, I tower over him,
I want to beat his ball,
but on the fairway, stormy, tired,
I follow his every move. Memorize.
This is what my father looks like
knocking the stuffing from a golf ball . . .
burned on all my eyes.

The swing, the pride. I can feel him
in my hands. A shot of sun.

5

Hugging another man, I feel myself:
ribs, sighs, sticky palms.
I walk into my father's arms afraid.

A blush, a bruise. Still solid, severe.
Standing his own ground,
not knowing when to close his eyes.

This is not a request for affection.
Nothing to reassure. This is a leap
from a windowsill, my father watching me fly.

We forget for a moment and bump,
good old male love.
There are handshakes in our timid hearts.

Stepping in, I throw myself around him,
tripped toes, a squeeze. His shoulder blades
almost collapse. We breathe.

His arms go up, a swoop.
He holds me for an instant,
a piece of the vast and falling sky.

ADAM AND INNOCENCE

In the beginning Adam was naive.
Playing names, fussing with
the breeze, pretending to be
a lion or a rock. Whatever
pleased. For God's keen eye
he hung from lower branches
in the shape and dangle of a fruit.
Posed naked on a cliff, a model
moon. The first experiment:
will he devise a language, be
seasonal, will he sink or swim?
Give of himself for the sake of
loneliness? He sat on the cold
hard ground and listened to
the sounds of everything. When
he spoke to streams, he believed
in their memory. Darkness
nothing more than a concealed face.

It is important for children
to learn to eat with forks, to
know that life is round, no Santa
Claus, the body covered up. I teach
little Adam he is neither an orange
nor Spiderman. Do not speak
to strangers, beware of promises.
A night-light glows in the nursery,
a plastic angel with a pink face.

Adam is always an innocent.
In the beginning children are never
reflections of ourselves. Wish
on a newborn, wish for a keen future.
Rather than die, wouldn't we all
choose to be rocks? Or moon about
the universe, like a bunch of angels
warming themselves on children's eyes.
To watch is a lonely occupation:
the inside wanting out. Adam and I
sit on the bedroom floor and I hear
every single sound he makes. I am
swayed by promises of memory. The
simple face beaming through
the shadows of my disbelief.